For Tom, David, and Peter M.W.

For Amy and Sandy B. F.

First U.S. edition 1996

Library of Congress Cataloging-in-Publication Data

Waddell, Martin.
You and me, Little Bear / Martin Waddell ;
illustrated by Barbara Firth. — 1st U.S. ed.
Summary: Little Bear helps Big Bear gather wood, fetch water,
and tidy the cave so that they can play together.
ISBN 1-56402-879-8
[1. Bears—Fiction. 2. Play—Fiction. 3. Helpfulness—Fiction.]
I. Firth, Barbara, ill.   II. Title.
PZ7.W1137Yo   1996
[E]—dc20   95-39342

2 4 6 8 10 9 7 5 3

Printed in Italy

This book was typeset in Columbus MT Semi-bold.
The pictures were done in pencil and watercolor.

Candlewick Press
2067 Massachusetts Avenue
Cambridge, Massachusetts 02140

YOU AND ME, LITTLE BEAR

Martin Waddell

illustrated by Barbara Firth

CANDLEWICK PRESS
CAMBRIDGE, MASSACHUSETTS

Once there were two bears,

Big Bear and Little Bear.

Big Bear is the big bear

and Little Bear is the little bear.

Little Bear wanted to play, but

Big Bear had things to do.

"I want to play!" Little Bear said.

"I have to get wood for the fire," said Big Bear.

"I'll get some, too," Little Bear said.

"You and me, Little Bear," said Big Bear.

"We'll bring the wood in together!"

"What shall we do now?" Little Bear asked.

"I'm going for water," said Big Bear.

"Can I come, too?" Little Bear asked.

"You and me, Little Bear," said Big Bear.

"We'll go for water together."

"Now we can play," Little Bear said.

"I still have to clean up our cave," said Big Bear.

"Well . . . I'll clean up, too!" Little Bear said.

"You and me," said Big Bear. "You clean up your things, Little Bear. I'll take care of the rest."

"I've cleaned up my things, Big Bear!"

Little Bear said.

"That's good, Little Bear," said Big Bear.

"But I'm not finished yet."

"I want you to play!" Little Bear said.

"You'll have to play by yourself,

Little Bear," said Big Bear. "I still

have plenty to do!"

Little Bear went to play by

himself, while Big Bear

continued with the work.

Little Bear played
bear-jump.

Little Bear

played

bear-slide.

Little Bear played
bear-swing.

Little Bear played
bear-tricks with bear-sticks.

Little Bear played bear-stand-on-his-head,

and Big Bear came out to sit on his rock.

Little Bear played bear-run-around-by-himself,

and Big Bear closed his

eyes to think.

Little Bear went to
talk to Big Bear,
but Big Bear was . . .

asleep!

"Wake up, Big Bear!" Little Bear said.

Big Bear opened his eyes.

"I've played all my games

by myself," Little Bear said.

Big Bear thought a minute, then he said,

"Let's play hide-and-seek, Little Bear."

"I'll hide and you seek," Little Bear said,

and he ran off to hide.

"Here I come!" Big Bear called, and he looked until he found Little Bear.

Then Big Bear hid, and Little Bear looked.

"I found you, Big Bear!" Little Bear said.

"Now I'll hide again."

They played lots of bear games.
When the sun slipped away through
the trees, they were still playing.
Then Little Bear said, "Let's go
home now, Big Bear."

Big Bear and Little Bear went

home to their cave.

"We've been busy today, Little Bear!"

said Big Bear.

"It was fun, Big Bear," Little Bear

said. "Just you and me playing . . .

together."